Mini Rabbit
IS
NOT
LOST

FOR
EVIE
&
OTTO
x

First published in English in Great Britain
by Harper Collins Children's Books,
a division of Harper Collins Publishers Ltd. under the title:
MINI RABBIT NOT LOST
Text and illustrations copyright © John Bond 2018
First published in the United State of America in 2019 by
Holiday House Publishing, Inc., New York

The author/illustrator asserts the moral right to be identified as the author/illustrator of the work.

Printed in China
1 3 5 7 9 10 8 6 4 2

Library of Congress Cataloging-in-Publication Data
Names: Bond, John, 1979– author, illustrator.
Title: Mini Rabbit is not lost / John Bond.
Description: First edition. | New York : Holiday House, 2019. | "Neal Porter
Books." | Originally published: London : HarperCollins Children's Books,
2018. | Summary: Mini Rabbit refuses all help and denies he is lost during
his epic quest to find more berries for the cake he and Mother Rabbit are making.
Identifiers: LCCN 2018049652 | ISBN 9780823443581 (hardcover)
Subjects: | CYAC: Lost children—Fiction. | Rabbits—Fiction. |
Baking—Fiction. | Humorous stories.
Classification: LCC PZ7.1.B662 Min 2019 | DDC [E]—dc23
LC record available at https://lccn.loc.gov/2018049652

Mini Rabbit

IS
NOT
LOST

JOHN BOND

NEAL PORTER BOOKS
HOLIDAY HOUSE / NEW YORK

Mini Rabbit and Mother Rabbit
are making a cake.

Mini Rabbit likes cake.

Caaaaake!

Oh dear, it looks like they've run out of berries.

No berries, no cake.

No cake?

No way!
I'll find berries.
Must have cake.

Come back,
Mini Rabbit!
There are some
under the . . .

Too late.
Mini Rabbit is
off to find berries.

Must have cake.

Cake! Cake! Cake!

I can find berries.

Looks like Mini Rabbit might
be going the wrong way.

Hello, Mini Rabbit.
Where are you going?
Do you need any help?

No, thank you.
Don't need help.
Looking for berries.
Making a cake.

Where could Mini Rabbit be going now?

Maybe this fellow can help
Mini Rabbit find berries?

Hello, Mini Rabbit.
It's pretty cold out here.
Don't you need
your coat?

No, no.
Not cold.
Looking for berries.
Making a cake.

Mini Rabbit has definitely gone the wrong way now...

And it looks very dangerous up here!

Mini Rabbit, STOP!
You're too small
to go down there,
aren't you?

No, no.
Not too small.
Looking for berries.
Making a . . .

Cake.

Cake . . .

Cake . . .

"

Not sure this is a good place for Mini Rabbit to find berries.

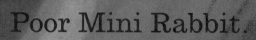

Poor Mini Rabbit.

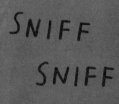

SNIFF
SNIFF

SNIFF

SNIFF

SNIFF

Hold on. What can Mini Rabbit smell?

SNIFF

SNIFF

SNIFF

Berry
cake
berry
cake
berry
cake...

I
found
a berry!

And I'm
going...

Mother Rabbit looks very pleased to see Mini Rabbit.

There you are!

I found a berry.

Well done,
Mini Rabbit.

Now, would you like
some cake?